BRONCO BUSTERS

ALISON CRAGIN HERZIG
KIMBERLY BULCKEN ROOT

G. P. PUTNAM'S SONS · NEW YORK

Text copyright © 1998 by Alison Cragin Herzig
Illustrations copyright © 1998 by Kimberly Bulcken Root
G. P. Putnam's Sons, a division of
The Putnam & Grosset Group, 200 Madison Avenue, New York, NY 10016.
G. P. Putnam's Sons, Reg. U.S. Pat. & Tm. Off. Published simultaneously in Canada.
Printed in Hong Kong by South China Printing Co.(1988) Ltd.
Book designed by Patrick Collins and Gunta Alexander. Text set in Administer.
Library of Congress Cataloging-in-Publication Data
Herzig, Alison Cragin. Bronco Busters / by Alison Cragin Herzig;
illustrated by Kimberly Bulcken Root.   p. cm.
Summary: Three rough, tough bronco busters can't tame a little black pony,
but a small, quiet cowboy talks to him and brings him water, and then
quietly rides away with him. [Horses—Training—Fiction. 2.Horses—Fiction.
3.Cowboys—Fiction.] I.Root, Kimberly Bulcken, ill. II.Title.
PZ7.H432478Br 1998 [E]—dc21 96-45329 CIP AC ISBN 0-399-22917-5
1 3 5 7 9 10 8 6 4 2
First Impression

For my father, Stuart Wilson Cragin,
and always for J. A. L. M. — A. C. H.

For Barry — K. B. R.

nce upon a time
there were three big bad bronco busters.
Their names were Slim, Jim and Grimsley.
Slim was rough, Jim was tough
and Grimsley was bowlegged.
In the whole wide West, they boasted,
there wasn't a bronco they couldn't bust.

One day they pulled into a ranch between
the tall grass prairie and the high blue mountains.
A small cowboy sat on the corral fence.
"Stand aside, sonny!" said Slim.
"We've come to break that little black bronco."

Slim strapped on spikey spurs
as big as pinwheels.
Jim and Grimsley uncoiled their lariats
and twirled the loops around their heads.
The black pony tried to run away.
But Jim lassoed him from the right.
Grimsley lassoed him from the left.
Slim slapped on a saddle and climbed aboard.
The black pony shivered and shook.

Then he reared and kicked and humped
and bucked all over the corral.
Slim went flying.
Jim and Grimsley hooted and hollered
and slapped their thighs.
Slim picked himself up off the ground
and hobbled away.

His spikey spurs
dragged in the dust.
"You call that bronco busting?"
Grimsley sneered.
"My turn tomorrow," said Jim.

And then the three bronco busters
went into the bunkhouse
to play cards and eat beef stew
and corn bread for supper.

That night, when everyone was asleep, the small cowboy
climbed back up on the corral fence to talk to the black pony.
He told him about the tickling grass on the prairie.
"It's taller than I am," he said, "and sometimes there are
buffalos." He told the pony about the cool, clear streams
that tumbled down the sides of the high blue mountains.
"We can camp out under the pine trees,"
he said, "and look for eagles."
The black pony edged closer.
The cowboy stroked the pony's forehead and rubbed
behind his ears.
The pony rested his head against the small cowboy's knees.

The next afternoon
the big bad bronco busters
swaggered out to the corral again.
"You still here, sonny?" said Slim.
"Let him stay," ordered Jim.
"He might learn a thing or two."
"Hi-i-i! Yi-i-i! Yah-h-h!" Slim yelled at the
black pony to show him who was boss.
Grimsley tied ropes to his front feet so that
every time he tried to run, he fell over.
Then, when the pony's sides were heaving
and he was lathered with sweat,
they slapped on a saddle.
Jim jammed his hat down to his eyebrows
and climbed aboard.

The pony bared his teeth.
He kicked and reared and twisted and twirled
and tried to climb the fence.
Jim went flying.
Grimsley hooted and hollered and slapped his thighs.
Jim picked his hat out of the dirt and limped away.

"Some bronc stomper you are," sneered Grimsley.
"He's a wild one," mumbled Jim.
"A real blind bucker," agreed Slim.

"We'll see about that," said Grimsley.
"It's my turn tomorrow."

Then they all went into the bunkhouse
to tell tall tales and eat hot dogs
and baked beans for supper.

That night, when everyone was asleep,
the small cowboy carried a pail of oats out to the corral.
He let the pony smell his hands and his face.
He filled his hat with water so the pony could drink.
He brushed the sweat off the pony's
neck and back with his lariat.
"I've brought my harmonica," he said.
"You want to hear me play?"
When it was time for the small cowboy to go,
the pony followed him to the gate
and watched until he was out of sight.

The next day the bronco busters
marched out to the corral again.
"The kid's still here," said Slim.
"Scram, pip-squeak!" said Jim.
"Yeah, beat it, squirt!" growled Grimsley.
"Let the big guys do it."

Slim tied the pony to a snubbing post.

Jim snuck up behind him
with the saddle.

Grimsley pulled his bandana over his face
to keep the dust out of his nose
and climbed aboard.

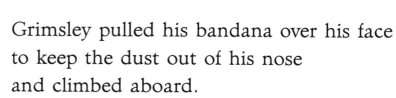

The pony bared his teeth
and rolled his eyes and
flattened his ears.
His hoofs flew in every
direction, but
Grimsley stayed on.

Slim and Jim cheered and whooped
and waved their hats.
Then the pony reared and kicked.

He humped and twisted
and twirled.
He jackknifed from one end
of the corral to the other.
Finally Grimsley went flying.
Slim and Jim stopped cheering.

They shook their heads and stared at their boots.
Grimsley dusted himself off and tottered away.
His bandana drooped around his neck.
"Told you," said Slim.
"He's a real outlaw," said Jim.

"Plum loco," muttered Grimsley.
"No one can ride that horse.
Nothing to do but sell him to the rodeo."
And then the three big bad bronco busters
climbed into their truck and drove away.

That night, when everyone was asleep,
the small cowboy came out of the ranch house.
He was loaded with gear.
The black pony whinnied softly
when he heard him coming.
The cowboy kissed the pony's velvety nose
and patted his back.
He showed him his bedroll.
"I packed peanut butter and jelly sandwiches for me,"
he whispered, "and apples and sugar lumps for you."
He showed him the bridle and the saddle blanket.
He let him smell the saddle before he put it on.
The pony stood quietly.
He listened to the gentle sound of the cowboy's voice.

The next morning the corral was empty and the gate was open.
Far out on the prairie the small cowboy rode the black pony
through the tall grass toward the high blue mountains.